SuperCat

vs the party pooper

Jeanne Willis

Illustrated by Jim Field

HarperCollins *Children's Books*

For Michael Wilcock, Superhero
J.W. xx

First published in Great Britain by HarperCollins Children's Books 2014
HarperCollins Children's Books is a division of HarperCollinsPublishers Ltd,
77-85 Fulham Palace Road, Hammersmith, London W6 8JB

Visit us on the web at
www.harpercollins.co.uk

SUPERCAT VS THE PARTY POOPER
Text copyright © Jeanne Willis 2014
Illustrations copyright © Jim Field 2014

Jeanne Willis and Jim Field assert the moral right to be identified
as the author and illustrator of this work.

2

ISBN 978-000-751865-4

Printed and bound in England by
Clays Ltd, St Ives plc

CONTENTS

Chapter One

TROUBLE AT THE PALACE

"**H**appy Birthday to you, Happy Birthday to you, Happy birthday, dear James, Happy Birthday to you!!!"

James Jones woke up to find his pet cat singing to him and waving a large gift under his nose.

This wasn't any old cat. This was Supercat.

"I wrapped your present with my own fair paws," he said proudly.

James sat up in bed and felt the package excitedly. It was soft and squashy. What on earth could it be?

Supercat had never given him a present when he was just an ordinary tabby called Tiger, but since the day he had eaten some strange fungus growing on one of James's filthy socks, everything had changed. Now he had superpowers.

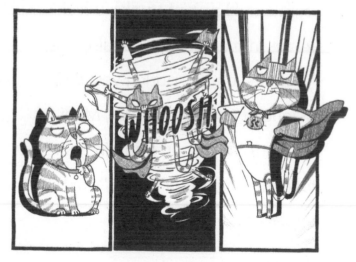

Not only could he sing, speak several languages and fight villains, he could also handle Sellotape. James tore off the wrapping.

"I designed it myself," said Supercat. "I hope it fits."

It was a superhero costume made from an old pair of trunks, which James immediately recognised as his dad's, and a sparkly vest that belonged to his little sister, Mimi.

"I based it on an outfit in your favourite *Tigerman* comic," said Supercat. "Try it on!"

James got out of bed, pulled on the costume over his pyjamas and looked in the mirror. The vest was so tiny it looked like a bra, and the trunks were so large that even with the drawstring pulled tight they bulged like a jester's pantaloons. He tried his best to sound delighted.

"Thank you, Supercat!" he said, struggling to find the right words. "It's... oh, it's..."

"Just what you always wanted!" beamed Supercat. "*C'est magnifique!* Now we've got matching superhero outfits. After all, we are a team."

"True," said James. "We defeated Count Backwards together, didn't we?"

At the mention of the mad mathematician's name, Supercat's fur stood on end.

"I'll never forget how he tried to destroy all the potatoes in the universe," he growled. "But the world can always count on us when the chips are down... Mmmmm... chips!"

James smiled. Some things never changed. Supercat might have the speed and strength of a lion, but he still had the stomach of the lazy old cat he used to be.

"Want some breakfast?" said James, stepping out of his outfit.

"Aren't you going to keep it on?" frowned Supercat.

James didn't want to disappoint his pet, but he couldn't go downstairs wearing that.

"I wish!" he said. "But I can't let Mimi see me dressed as a superhero.

If she finds out we're crime fighters, she'll tell Mum and Dad. It'll ruin everything."

"Good thinking," said Supercat, striding out of the room like a man. "Race you down there... I want to watch you open the rest of your presents."

James gave him a gentle reminder.

"Remember to behave like Tiger in front of the family. No walking on two legs, OK?"

Supercat sighed, dropped on to all fours and followed James downstairs.

All in all, James was very pleased with his birthday presents. Among other things, he'd got some new trainers, a leather football

and a deluxe chemistry set from his

grandma and grandpa, complete with

a set of goggles.

He couldn't wait to mix the sachets of powder together to see how they'd react. Hoping for a spectacular

ING

he was about to get the test tubes out of the box when his mum handed him a red envelope.

19

"Here's your big present," she said. "From me and Dad."

"*I* want a present!" sulked Mimi, thumping the kitchen table with her fists.

"It's not your birthday," said James. "It's mine and the Queen's."

James liked having the same birthday as the Queen – it made him feel important – but it was the last thing Mimi wanted to hear.

"Why isn't it *my* birthday?" she scowled, kicking him under the table. "I want my birthday *now*!"

Normally, James would have pulled Mimi's plaits and told her to stop being a brat, but he didn't want to get told off on his birthday, so he ignored her and opened the envelope instead. His eyes lit up. Inside was a ticket for London Zoo.

"It's not just any old ticket,"
said Mum. "You get to follow the
zookeeper for a whole day and feed
the animals, including the lions and
tigers."

"Brilliant!" said James. "Thanks!"

He was very fond of animals – especially tigers. His favourite comic superhero was Tigerman and Supercat's 'pet name' was Tiger too.

"Not fair! *I* want to feed the tigers!" moaned Mimi.

"We're all going to the zoo as a family, Mimi," explained Mum.

James rolled his eyes.

"How come Mimi gets to gatecrash my birthday treat?" he complained. "She'd better not come near me when I'm feeding the tigers. I'll throw her into the den."

Mimi screamed so
loudly that Supercat
had to stuff his paws
in his ears.

"Shh!" said Dad. "I'm trying to catch the news. Something very odd has happened at Buckingham Palace."

He turned up the radio.

"Reports are coming in that during the Queen's birthday feast, which began at dawn, Her Majesty, the royal family and all her guests, including the Prime Minister, the US President and the top man from the Ministry of Defence, all went down with a mysterious sleeping sickness..."

"Good heavens," said Mum. "I

wonder what caused it?"

"Oysters?" said Supercat, forgetting he wasn't meant to speak.

James sneezed loudly to cover it up, but Mimi had heard and was staring at Supercat in amazement.

"Tiger spoke!" she said.

James shook his head and sneezed loudly again.

"Ahh... snoyster!" he said.

"Shh!" said Dad. "They're interviewing Baron C Duckswat. Apparently he's the only party guest who's still awake and the only

person who knows what's going on.
The press aren't allowed inside the
palace in case the sleeping sickness
is catching."

"Baron C Duckswat?" said Mum.
"I've never heard of him."

"I expect he's from Europe," said
Dad. "The Queen invites guests from
around the globe. The King of Tonga
is there too. I had him in my cab
once."

"Quiet a minute," said Mum. "Let's
hear what the Baron has to say."

The Baron certainly sounded

foreign. He had a very unusual accent
– *almost as if he was putting it on*,
thought James.

"...Zis is Baron C Duckswat. I em
calling to inform you zat Her Majesty
and guests hev been taken to ze

palace hospital ving, vere zey are

being taken care of by ze royal doctors

until zey vake up. Meanvile, as ze only

man standing, I vill be your new King!"

James's parents exchanged worried glances.

"He can't just appoint himself King, can he?" said Mum.

"If the entire royal family and the Prime Minister are asleep, I suppose he can do what the heck he likes," said Dad. "But I don't like the sound of him much."

Dad wasn't the only one.

"I've got a nasty feeling about this, Supercat," whispered James. "We must be prepared."

Supercat gave him a secret thumbs

up with his new thumbs as James gathered his presents and got down from the table.

"Mum, we'll still be able to go to the zoo today, won't we?" he said.

"Yes, I should think so," she said. "Go and get ready. And you, Mimi."

James did as he was told. But he had no intention of staying at the zoo. Somehow, he had to get to Buckingham Palace – and fast!

The question was how could he take Supercat with him?

Chapter Two

TOILET TROUBLE

"**H**urry up and get in the car, James," said his mum. "We don't want to miss the train."

"Won't be a sec," he said. "Just doing up my backpack."

It was so full, one of the seams had split. He was struggling to close it.

"Breathe in,
Supercat!"
he whispered.
"Keep your
head down."

James heaved the bag into the
back of his dad's cab and sat as far
away from Mimi as possible. But it
wasn't far enough.

"James, why is your back pack wriggling?" she asked.

"It isn't. It's just moving because Dad started the engine."

For a second, Mimi fell silent. Then she started up again.

"There's a stripy tail sticking out of your backpack!"

The tail was now swishing. James gulped, tucked it back in and tried to laugh it off.

"It's not a tail, you ninny," he said. "It's my jumper sleeve."

Mimi pulled a face. It was obvious

she didn't believe him, and as the car pulled away she leaned over and poked the bag. Supercat let out a startled miaow.

"Mum? Mum! James's backpack is miaowing!" said Mimi.

Trust her to let the cat out of the bag.

"It's not miaowing!" said James. "Mimi's ears need washing."

But everyone had heard. Dad stopped the car.

"James, you can't bring Tiger to the zoo! Pets aren't allowed," said Mum.

James had known it was going to be tricky sneaking Supercat in the car and on to the train, but how else was he going to get him to Buckingham Palace?

"Put him back indoors, now," said Mum. "He wouldn't enjoy it. All he wants to do is eat and sleep."

Reluctantly, James undid his backpack, scooped out Supercat and carried him back to the garden.

Supercat was furious.

"All I want to do is eat and sleep? Your mother has got me so wrong!" he said. "I don't want to *sleep*, I have a crime to solve. My country needs me!"

"And so do I," said James. "Is there any chance you could use your superpowers to follow the car and meet me on the train without Mimi spotting you?"

Supercat struck a heroic pose in the flower bed.

"*Mais oui!*" he said. "There's *every* chance. You go on ahead, I will give it a few minutes, then with the speed of a cheetah and the cunning of a leopard, I will race you to the station. I might even beat you..."

"Meet me on the train in Loo HQ,

Carriage P at 12.30," said James,
hurrying back up the garden path.
"And Supercat?"

"*Si?*"

"Mind the roads."

"Don't you worry about me,
my friend! I have nine lives," said
Supercat, falling

backwards

over the

garden gnome.

"Wahhh...

make that

eight."

Luckily, nothing was hurt apart
from his pride. Supercat lay on the
grass and waited for James and
his family to drive away.

For a moment,
he drifted off and
was just having
a lovely dream
about fish fingers

when the sound of the car engine
woke him with a start.

Bleary eyed from his catnap,
he leaped up and raced after
it as it cruised round the corner.

WHOOSH

Keeping a low profile,

he followed it into the market square,

pumping his furry legs so fast, the
tarmac melted on the road.

"Tiger Power, rargh, rargh, rargh!"
he roared.

To his surprise, the car parked at
the supermarket. An old lady got out
and paid the driver and it was then
that Supercat realised his mistake –
he'd followed the wrong cab! Even
worse, the station was on the other
side of town.

Blowing on his scorching paws to cool them down, he took a deep breath and ran off in the opposite direction, weaving in and out of the traffic. The directions were well signposted and as Supercat could read, he had no trouble getting to the station. **TRAIN STATION**

However, he arrived just as the guard was blowing his whistle and by the time Supercat reached the platform, the last carriage was disappearing into a tunnel.

As the train hurtled down the track, James sat with his family in Carriage Q, and busied himself with a notebook and pencil. He was trying to work something out, but Mimi kept kicking him under the table. James glanced at his watch. It was almost 12.30 – time to meet Supercat.

"Just going to the loo," he said.

James made his way to Carriage P and waited for Supercat in the corridor by the toilets.

And he waited. And he waited.

It wasn't like Supercat to be late.

Maybe he was in Loo HQ already?
It was locked – the engaged sign
was on. He tapped on the door.

"Are you in there, Supercat?" he
whispered.

The toilet flushed, the door swished
open and a huge man with a bald
head and
bulging biceps
came out.

"Are you
taking the
mick?" he
scowled.

"Sorry, I thought you were my friend," said James.

"Do I look like I've got any friends?" he growled. "Get out the way."

James pressed himself against the window and let him pass. He opened the window and leaned out, looking for Supercat. He was really anxious now.

James looked at his watch again. Perhaps it was running slow? He peered out of the window again. He was just hoping something dreadful hadn't happened when out of the corner of his eye, he saw a furry blur

hurtling
down the
track like a
ball of tabby
tumbleweed.

"Supercat!" he called.

"*Bonjour!*" puffed Supercat. "Sorry
I'm a... bit late, got... a... blister!"

He was falling behind.

James reached out

his hand.

"Keep running!"
he yelled. "You're
nearly there... give
me your paw."

Supercat tried to
grab hold.

"Your legs are too
short!" said James.

"No, your arms
are too short!" said
Supercat.

James whipped
off his belt and hung
it out of the window.

"Grab hold!" he said. "You can do it!"

Supercat made one last effort; his little dumpling feet went into overdrive. The train tracks were in danger of warping.

"Now!" said James.

Supercat pounced on the belt and caught it in his claws. James held on to the other end, leaned back and gave a mighty heave. After much scrabbling, Supercat flew through the window and landed inside the train with a *plop*.

"Thank goodness you made it!" said James. "I've got something really important to tell you. Let's hurry to Loo HQ!"

Once they were safely inside the toilet cubicle, James locked the door and pulled out his notebook.

"Look at this," he said.

Supercat gazed at the page. It was covered in the letters of the alphabet that appeared in the name 'Baron C Duckswat'. James had swivelled the letters around several times to try and make new names.

B-A-R-O-N C D-U-C-K-S-W-A-T

R-O-N-A B B C-A-C-K-D-R-A-W-S

K-U-R-T S-W-A-N-D-B-A-C-C-O

"I don't get it," said Supercat.

"Nor did I... at first," said James.
"But all will be revealed."

James turned over the page. As
soon as Supercat read the name that
was spelled out, his hackles went up.

"C-O-U-N-T B-A-C-K-W-A-R-D-S!"

"Correct!' said James. "Count
Backwards and Baron C Duckswat
are the same person. He has simply

55

disguised his name so no one knows who's really behind the bad business at Buckingham Palace!"

"The swine!" said Supercat, stamping accidentally on the floor button, which made the cold tap squirt him in the face. "I thought we'd seen the back of the Count when I shot down his helicopter over the river.

However did he get away?"

"Maybe he has a submarine," said James.

"We must go after him and halt his evil plan, whatever it may be!" said Supercat, punching the air and setting  off the hand dryer, which blasted his fur into a lopsided quiff.

He stood on the pedal bin to look in the mirror.

"Lend me your comb, James," he said.

"I haven't got a comb! I'm a ten-year-old boy," said James.

Supercat did his best to pat down his fur and straighten his whiskers. Pleased with his appearance, he went to sit down but the toilet seat was up and his furry bottom disappeared down the bowl. Flailing around wildly, he almost

58

flushed himself away, but James
pulled him out and patted him dry
with a paper towel, trying hard not
to giggle.

"Right, well, it's lucky you packed
our costumes," said Supercat, acting
as if nothing had happened. "Not only
will I have something dry to put on,
we'll be dressed for action!"

James opened his bag.

"I only packed yours," he said.

Supercat looked inside. There was
only one superhero outfit – a cat-sized
one with a tail hole in the back of the

pants. It was a new costume he'd
made to replace the one that had
got ruined the last time he met Count
Backwards.

"Oh," he said. "Did you forget to
bring yours?"

"As if I could do that!" James
smiled, unzipping his jacket. He was
wearing his outfit underneath his
clothes. Supercat could see he had
the pants on too, by the way his
jeans ballooned around his backside.

"I can't wear my costume on the
outside," said James. "If people see it,

they'll know I'm up to something."

"I can wear mine though, can't I?" said Supercat. "I am the Hidden Claw! The Padded Paw! No one knows I'm here..."

"Let's try and keep it that way," said James. "Hide in Loo HQ until the next station. It's only a short walk to the zoo from there. Follow us without Mimi seeing and meet me by the tiger enclosure at two o'clock."

"OK," said Supercat, posing in his costume. "How do I look?"

"Like a hero," said James. "Only

your pants are inside out."

As Supercat adjusted his bottom half, James went back to his seat.

"You've been gone a long time," said Mum. "I was beginning to worry."

"Got a bit of tummy trouble," fibbed James. "It must be all the excitement."

And as the train pulled into Camden Town, things were about to get even more exciting.

Chapter Three

THE BIG BANG

"My legs ache!" moaned Mimi as they walked towards the zoo. "Daddy, you said it wasn't far. Carry me!"

"You're such a baby," said James as his father picked her up.

Mimi leaned over her father's

shoulder and stuck out her tongue.

Then suddenly her expression

changed. She was waving and

pointing down the road.

"Look! I can see Tiger!" she said.

James whisked round. Sure enough, Supercat was hovering by an ice-cream van, sniffing the air.

"That's not Tiger, you nutcase," he said. "Mum, Mimi needs glasses."

"Stop arguing," said Dad. "We're nearly there. I can see the sign for the zoo."

There was a long queue to get in. But not with James's ticket.

"You can go straight to the front with that, James," said Dad. "Just give your ticket to the zookeeper there."

The zookeeper was surrounded by

a group of children clutching similar red envelopes.

"Off you go," said Mum. "We'll meet you by the main gift shop at six."

"Yes, go," said Mimi, sticking out her tongue again.

"James Jones, is it?" said the zookeeper as James walked over. "Right, that's everyone on my list. Follow me! First stop, we're off to feed the penguins."

It was great fun posting wet mackerel into the penguins' enclosure.

It was even more fun watching the python swallow a dead rat in the reptile house. James was beginning to wish he could stay there all day, but someone had to save the Queen.

"And now for the big cats!" announced the zookeeper.

As they left the reptile house, James could hear loud roaring. It was a scary sound, so deep and rumbly he could feel the vibrations through the soles of his new trainers. He hoped Supercat wasn't frightened, all on his own.

"We'll feed the lions first," said the zookeeper, attaching a lump of raw meat to a pointed stick. "Just don't look them in the eye or put your fingers through the bars."

James waited until the zookeeper's back was turned and sidled off towards the tiger enclosure. There were no visitors there – they'd all rushed over to watch the lions being fed. It was just as well, because when he arrived, Supercat was showing off in front of a female tiger by doing press-ups on one paw.

James tried to attract his attention.

"Psst... Supercat? Time to go!"

"Can't you see I'm busy?" said
Supercat.

It took James some time to drag him away.

"What were you *thinking* of, Supercat?" said James. "You were in full view of the zoo!"

"I was thinking of giving Rani my phone number."

"Rani will never call you," said James.

Supercat sucked in his stomach and puffed out his chest.

"She will," he said. "I'm witty, I'm handsome. How can she resist me?"

"Tigers don't have telephones,"

said James.

Supercat wasn't the brightest of cats, but his heart was in the right place, so James did his best not to make him feel foolish.

"We can always come back to the zoo and see her again," he said. "But right now we have to focus on our mission and get to Buckingham Palace."

James pulled out a map of the London Underground.

"We have to take the tube to Green Park, come on."

Keeping their heads down, James
and Supercat hurried out of the zoo
and made their way to Camden Town
tube station.

Supercat had never been on the
Underground before, and having
been clapped in the face by the ticket
barrier he was already dazed and
confused by the time he hit
the escalator.

"Help!" he squealed,
clinging to the handrail
and pedalling his
paws frantically.

"The stairs are moving!"

"They're meant to move," said James. "Stand still and relax."

It was good advice until they got near the bottom. As the escalator stairs flattened out and mysteriously disappeared under a row of metal teeth, Supercat freaked out. Terrified that he was going to be swallowed alive, he hastily reversed up the stairs and bumped into a businessman holding a briefcase. It sprang open, scattering assorted pens, paper and a packed lunch far and wide.

"Cats should be carried on the escalator!" shouted the man, scrabbling after a satsuma, which was bouncing down the steps.

"He's not my cat," said James as they both ran towards the platform.

"I don't care whose cat he is, he stood on my cheese roll!" bellowed the man.

James and Supercat jumped on to the waiting train and the doors closed. Then they opened again. Then they closed. Then they opened.

"What's the hold-up?" said
Supercat.

"Someone must have got their coat
caught in the doors," grumbled James.

"What kind of idiot would do that?"
tutted Supercat. "We might as well sit
down."

Only he couldn't. Something held
him back. The more he struggled, the
more he was being strangled where
he stood.

"Your cloak," said James. "It's stuck."

He tugged it back through the
rubber seal on the doors, which flew

open, banged shut and finally the
train departed.

There was a newspaper left on
an empty seat. To avoid the gaze of
the other passengers, James grabbed
it and they hid behind the pages,
pretending to read. They did the same
thing when they changed on to the
Victoria Line.

"This train goes all the way to Green Park," whispered James, behind the *Daily Mail*.

"Hmm?" said Supercat. "Sorry, I'm just reading this very interesting article..."

"Is it about the Queen?" whispered James, hoping for an update on the royal situation.

Supercat rubbed his tummy.

"No. It's about food. I could eat a horse."

"Maybe if we rescue the Queen, she'll give us party nibbles," said

James. "Sausages on sticks and stuff."

The train arrived at Green Park. They got out, followed the signs to Buckingham Palace and made their way to the entrance gate.

"It's a magnificent monument, isn't it?" said James.

"I don't like the look of that at all," growled Supercat.

James was surprised.

"You don't like the palace?"

"I was talking about the monstrosity next to it," said Supercat.

James squinted in the bright

sunlight. Now that Supercat had pointed it out, he could see a strange little building among the trees next to the palace. He recognised it immediately. The building was no wider than a caravan, a bit shorter than a house and it had turrets and flags decorated with numbers – five, four, three, two, one.

"It's Count Backwards' mobile castle!" said James. "We got trapped inside it when he drove it to his weevil-bomb factory!"

"We defeated him then and we'll defeat him now," said Supercat, running through the golden gates towards the palace.

James dashed after him.

"Wait, Supercat... How are we going to get past the guards?"

Supercat screeched to a halt and stared at the men in scarlet uniforms and furry hats.

"*Quelle horreur!* They're wearing stuffed cats on their heads!" he spluttered.

"It's OK. They're bearskin," said James.

Supercat narrowed his eyes.

"It's not OK if you're a bear," he said. "And I'll tell you another thing, those are not the Queen's guards."

"They look like them to me," said James.

But Supercat's super-vision told him otherwise.

"They have numbers painted on their boots. We've come up against these boys before. They're members of the Calculator Crew!"

"Count Backwards' henchmen?" said James.

Supercat spat on the grass.

"Yes, they are none other than Mr Plus and Mr Minus!"

To Supercat's surprise, James calmly got his chemistry set out of his backpack.

"You won't distract them by making crystals and funny smells," scoffed Supercat.

James put on his protective goggles.

"I'm going to make an explosion," he said. "Follow me."

Chapter Four

LET THEM EAT CAKE

Unseen by Mr Plus and Mr Minus, James and Supercat crept up behind their sentry box and set up the test-tube rack. It wasn't the first chemistry set James had owned, but it was easily the best. The ingredients were extremely powerful and as he mixed the yellow powder with the purple liquid, it began to pour with smoke. Supercat read the warning on the box: *Keep away from children*. He grabbed the test tube from James.

"I'll handle this!" he said. "You may be seventy in cat years, but you are still a child."

"Look out, it's about to blow!" said James.

Supercat held the tube to his nose and gave it a sniff.

"Really? I'd give it a few beats. It doesn't look as if it's going to make a very loud..."

The explosion almost blew his

whiskers off.

"Whoa!!! Are you OK?" said James.

Thankfully, Supercat was still in one piece – the bang was worse than the blast, but it put the wind up the calculators.

"Did you hear that explosion? Was it you, Mr Plus?" said Mr Minus.

"No, I thought it was *you*, Mr Minus," said Mr Plus.

Thinking they were under attack, the guards threw themselves face down on to the grass.

SQUELCH

"Bomb! Hit the deck, Mr Plus!" said Mr Minus.

"I already have, Mr Minus," said Mr Plus, "but don't tell the Count!"

James and Supercat tiptoed past
them and slipped into the palace.
There was a huge mirror in the hall.
Supercat looked at his reflection and

gasped. His
eyebrows
were singed,
his nose was
sooty and his
fur was sticking

out in spikes like a horse chestnut.

"Holy cape!" he wailed.

"Is that your new catchphrase?"
asked James.

Supercat shook his head sadly.

"No, I have a hole in my cape."

James gave him a friendly squeeze.

"It'll mend. I'm just glad you're all right, Supercat."

"I will be when I've beaten Count Backwards," he said. "Nothing can stop me!"

He spoke too soon. As Supercat charged up the stairs to find the Queen, a pack of corgis appeared out of nowhere and tried to chase him back down. It was impossible to fend them off with ninja kicks – they

kept nipping
his ankles –
so he did a
super-leap,
grabbed
hold of a
chandelier
and tried
to swing
away.

Unfortunately, one of the corgis had already sunk its teeth into the back of his cloak and refused to let go.

The weight
of the corgi was
about to bring him
and the chandelier
crashing to the
floor when James
yelled, "Catch!"
and threw him
a sword from a
suit of armour at
the foot of the
staircase.

Supercat caught
it in his teeth, sliced
through the hem of
his cloak and the dog
fell through the air on
to the sofa below.

"Bad dog, sit!" said Supercat triumphantly.

He dropped on to the banister and, waving his sword like a musketeer, he drove the rest of the dogs downstairs and James shut them in the toilet.

"And now we must go to the Banqueting Hall!" said Supercat.

"Why?" said James. "Is that where you think the Count will be?"

"Maybe, and we might find some sausages on sticks," said Supercat."

James smiled. Not only had Supercat's new powers given him the strength of a lion and the speed of a cheetah, they'd given him the appetite of an elephant.

"I guess we might as well start there, then," he said.

But there were so many rooms it

was anybody's guess where the feast had been held.

"I bet it's that one," said James, pointing to a door with a bunch of balloons pinned on to it. He looked through the keyhole to make sure no one was inside and pushed it open.

"How did you know? Your psychic skills amaze me," said Supercat, gazing in delight at the enormous table covered with party blowers, silly string and half-eaten food. There were sausages on sticks, crisps, pizza and, right in the middle, a massive birthday cake with six tiers. The top tier had already been cut, but there was a slice left. Supercat licked his lips, sat down and grabbed it. He was about to take a bite when James snatched it away.

"Don't eat it!" he said. "Mystery illness, my foot! I reckon Count Backwards put something in that cake to make the guests fall asleep."

"The Party Pooper!" said Supercat. "Why didn't he want them awake?"

"So he could crown himself King," said James. "Kings have power over the whole country. I hate to think what he's going to do with it."

Just then, he noticed that Supercat's ears were swivelling.

"What is it?" said James. "What can you hear?"

"A cry for help," said Supercat, bounding off towards the kitchen. He burst through the swing doors and looked around. There was no one there.

"Never fear, Supercat is here!" he announced.

"Where's here?" came a muffled voice.

"By the fridge," Supercat replied. "Where are you?"

"Locked in the larder," said another voice.

Supercat took a few steps back.

"Don't worry. I'll soon have you out!"

He did a spectacular run-up and was about to hurl himself against the door when James handed him the larder key.

"It was in the fruit bowl," he said. "I'd use it if I were you. You don't want to get splinters."

Supercat unlocked the door. The palace chef, the cooks and several waiters came tumbling out. To his surprise, they were only wearing pants and vests.

"I expect it gets very hot in the kitchen," said James.

The head waiter wrapped a tea towel round his waist to cover his baggy Y-fronts.

"It's not the heat," he said. "The

Calculator Crew stole our uniforms. They dressed up as waiters and served cake to all the guests."

"Count Backwards crushed sleeping pills into it," added the chef.

James and Supercat exchanged knowing glances.

"It's just as we suspected," said Supercat. "Count Backwards wants to have his cake and eat it!"

The chef shook his head violently.

"No, he wanted everyone *else* to eat it. We tried to stop him, but the Calculators overpowered us. Do you know where they have taken Her Royal Highness? Is the Prime Minister awake? And the royal baby? Mind you, I expect the princess will be glad if he's gone to sleep – he's a bit of a screamer."

James was about to tell him what he'd heard on the news when he was interrupted by a deafening noise. It was so loud, it made his ears ring. It was as if a madman had got hold of a dinner gong and was trying to kill it with a hammer. Suddenly, the kitchen doors flew open. Supercat shot under the table.

"Five, four three, two, one really shouldn't *BONG*!! gossip with the *BONG*!! royal staff, James!" said Count Backwards. "Whatever are *you* doing here?"

The Count was standing in the doorway, banging an enormous dinner gong held by Mr Plus and Mr Minus. The kitchen staff took one look at the Calculators and shut themselves back in the larder.

"What are *you* doing here, Count Backwards?" said James. "It's not your party. It's the Queen's."

The Count tossed his crazy white hair.

"I'm the King! King trumps queen. It's *my* party now."

He sprang like a mad rat and

grabbed James around the throat.

"My cake went down a bomb!" he tittered. "Talking of which, somebody tried to blow up my Calculators earlier. When I find out who it was, I will have them for pudding. "

"It was me!" said Supercat, threatening him from behind with a frying pan.

Count Backwards let go of James and spun round. Seeing his furry enemy, he did a ridiculous little dance, then singing in a spooky voice, he stalked Supercat round the kitchen table.

"Pussycat, pussycat where have you been?"

"I've been to London to visit the Queen..." said Supercat. "Not that it's any of your business."

Seeing that the Count was driving Supercat towards the Calculators, who were stalking him in the other direction, James stood in his way.

"Back off, Backwards!"

"Five, four, three, two, one – zero chance!" bellowed the Count. "I will fight you and your tubby tabby to the bitter end, Master Jones! Choose your weapons *now*!"

He grabbed the electric food mixer, turned it on full blast and, spraying them with cake mixture, he chased James and Supercat back into the Banqueting Hall.

Chapter Five

PARTY GAMES

The flex on the food mixer was short and having pulled out the plug, Backwards found himself without a weapon. Suddenly the tables had turned and, to his horror, James was advancing on him with a balloon.

"No... no! Don't pop it!" he cringed.

"I hate it when they go bang."

"Good," said James, bursting it loudly with a fork.

Count Backwards shrieked in terror and leaped back. Then, furious at having been made to look a fool, he

felt around for a plate of sausages,

hoping to poke James with the

cocktail stick. Too late! Supercat had

pulled them all out and was firing

them at the Count's bottom with an

elastic band.

"Bullseye!" he whooped. "You should have worn your lucky pants, Backwards."

The Count clutched his sore behind.

"If I wear them backwards, they rub!" he shrieked, trying to protect his backside with a tea tray. The Calculators leaped to his defence.

"Use your loaf, sire!" said Mr Plus. "Pelt them with sandwiches!"

He chose a salmon and cucumber one and lobbed it as hard as he could at James. It flew over his head and landed on the grand piano.

"You hit a bum note there!" said James, picking up a whole pizza and throwing it at Mr Plus like a frisbee. It hit him in the face cheesy-side down and stuck there. Unable to see through the dough, the Calculator blundered around blindly, skidded on some jelly and fell head first into the umbrella stand.

"This is no time to get your head down, Mr Plus," said Mr Minus. "This is the best fight since sliced bread."

He picked up a jam sandwich and hurled it at Supercat. It missed him by a whisker. Supercat brushed the crumbs off his shoulder.

"I prefer mine with the crusts on," he said, releasing a volley of meringues, which shattered on the Calculator's suit and showered him with pink sugar.

"Look out, Supercat!" warned James as Mr Plus crept up with a soda siphon.

Supercat grabbed a bottle of fizzy lemonade. Giving it a super-feline shake, he pointed it at Mr Plus, undid the lid and squirted him in the face – *Pshhhhhhh!*

"Ugh! I'm all *sticky*, Mr Minus," groaned Mr Plus.

"Ugh, I'm all *crispy,* Mr Plus," moaned Mr Minus as James jumped on to the table and emptied a bumper bag of cheesy puffs down his trousers.

As the Calculators spat on the napkins to clean themselves up, Count Backwards seized a glass bowl loaded with custard, jelly and sponge and chucked it at Supercat.

"Disposing of you will be a mere trifle!" he cackled.

The bowl sailed through the air, then crashed to the floor and shattered, narrowly missing Supercat and James, who had ducked behind the sideboard. The Count was so busy buffing blobs of custard off his new shoes, he didn't see where they had hidden.

"Five, four, three, two, one-der where they've gone?" he muttered as he straightened up.

He scanned the room – there was no sign of them.

"Drat!" he said, thumping the table so hard that all the cutlery shot up in the air. Just then, he spotted the party bags.

"Aha! What do we have here?"

Rummaging through them and with

a delighted squeak, he found a tiny plastic magnifying glass and held it up to one eye.

"Come out, come out, wherever you are!" he sang. "If you want to play party games, I'm very good at hide-and-seek..."

"I'd rather play pass the parcel, Mr Plus," muttered Mr Minus.

"Or musical bumps, Mr Minus," mouthed Mr Plus. "But don't tell the Count!"

The Count picked up a party trumpet, stood in the middle of the room and closed his eyes.

"I am going to count to ten, then when I blow my tooter we're coming to find you!"

The Calculators tried hard to hide their disappointment.

"Are *we* playing too? Isn't that great, Mr Plus?" simpered Mr Minus.

"Indeed, Mr Minus. Hide-and-seek is our favourite," fawned Mr Plus. "Nice tooter, Your Highness!"

"One, two, three, four, five..." counted Backwards, forwards.

Supercat and James huddled together out of sight, hatching a plan.

"Is the Count going to toot us to death?" whispered Supercat. "I'm sick of him blowing his own trumpet."

James peered round the sideboard.

"No... he's gone for the bottle of squeezy ketchup," said James.

"The little squirt!" said Supercat,

holding up a bag of party poppers. "Let's attack!"

James held him back.

"We're outnumbered. We must use the element of surprise. Keep your paw on your poppers and when I say 'fire', we'll drive them all up against the wall."

Supercat scooped up his ammo and sat tight.

"Seven, eight, nine, ten... toot! Coming to get you, ready or not!" said the Count.

He began to comb the room with

the Calculators, looking inside the grandfather clock, checking behind the curtains, hunting under the table. They were getting nearer and nearer. Supercat couldn't hold back any longer.

"Let me at him!" he growled.

"OK, let's do it while they're backs are turned," said James. "Fire!"

They charged out from behind the sideboard.

"Tiger Power, rargh rargh rargh!" roared Supercat,

Pop-pop-pop-pop-pop-pop-pop-pop-pop!

James grabbed a can of silly string
and as Supercat rounded up the
shocked Calculators, he cornered
Count Backwards.

"It's dangerous to point those
things at people," he cowered. "Stop
or I'll tell your mother!"

"Never!" said James, waving the can at him. "Not until you tell us your evil plan!"

The Count shook his head.

"Nope!"

"Fine, have it your way," said James. "Burst the balloons, Supercat!"

Supercat grabbed a bunch of balloons, pinged out his middle claw and popped one.

BANG!

The Count screamed, crouched down and clamped his hands over his ears.

"Don't burst them!" he squealed.

"Talk, then!" said James.

The Count put his thumb in his mouth and rocked as he spoke.

"I have crowned myself King," he pouted, "so I can change all the rules.

Rule number five, four, three, two, one – all cats must be thrown in the river and drownded."

"Drownded?" exclaimed Supercat.

"Yes!' said Count Backwards. "It's payback time. Last time we met, you shot me down in my helicopter and I almost drownded. Now it's your turn, Poopercat."

James looked at him in disgust.

"There is no such word as drownded. You can't even speak the Queen's English."

The Count pulled out his thumb

with a plop.

"But I'm a genius at sums," he said. "I worked for the Secret Ser—"

"I know," said James.

"It's *rude to* interrupt," tutted the Count. "I solved the hardest sum in the world to crack a code, but the cleaner unplugged my computer before I could save the answer, and..."

Supercat yawned. It was a great story, but he'd heard it all before.

"We KNOW," he said. "You went mad and the Secret Service fired you."

Count Backwards' eyes filled with hatred.

"I will get my revenge on them!" he screeched. "Their leader sleeps in the hospital wing along with the US President. I will take over England, then America, then the world and the man from the Secret Service won't be able to stop me... hee hee heeeeee!"

James had heard enough. He pressed the nozzle on the silly string and squirted the Count with it until the can was empty. As Backwards tried to tear silly string out of his silly hair,

Supercat ran rings around
him with a length of
birthday bunting, until
he was wrapped
from neck to ankle
like a festive mummy
in hundreds of little
flags printed with the
Union Jack.

"Help me, boys!" he
cried. "Divide and conquer! Multiply
your efforts!"

The Calculators stuck out their feet
in an effort to trip Supercat up.

"Put your right leg in, Mr Plus," said Mr Minus.

"Put your left leg out, Mr Minus," said Mr Plus. "In out, in out. Shake it all about."

It was useless. Supercat was spinning too fast. As the Calculators tried to kick his paws from under him, they slipped on the spilt trifle, banged their heads together and were knocked out cold.

"Tie them up with balloon ribbon before they come round, Supercat," said James. "Leave the Count to me."

By now Backwards had toppled on to the rug like a skittle. He was unable to move but he could still yell.

"You won't get away with this, Supercat!" he screamed. "I will be King! I will take over the world! You can't stop me!"

James knelt down and pinched the Count's nostrils together until he opened his mouth.

"Time for a taste of your own medicine," he said, cramming it with birthday cake. "Don't have nightmares."

Backwards struggled for a second, swallowed, then, blinking sleepily, he shoved his thumb in his mouth and closed his eyes. James waited for a few moments, then pinched his cheek to make sure that he was in a deep sleep.

"He's out for the count," he said. "But let's not count our chickens..."

"I already have, and there's only one leg left. Sorry..." said Supercat, gnawing away at the drumstick of roast meat in his fist.

"We'll come back for that

134

drumstick and deal with Count Backwards later," said James. "Right now, we need to find the hospital wing and save the Queen."

Chapter Six

THE ROYAL WEE

"**B**uckingham Palace is even bigger on the inside than the outside," grumbled Supercat as he and James searched for the Queen.

They had been wandering for ages, and so far they'd found the Ballroom, the Hat Room, the Medal Room, the

Lego Room, the Post Room and the

Boiler Room – but no hospital.

"Perhaps the hospital wing is

behind this door," said James.

Wrong again. They were in the Queen's bedroom. Supercat lay down on the four-poster bed next to the royal teddy and closed his eyes. "No sleeping on the job," said James. "You didn't eat some of that cake, did you?"

"I didn't touch a crumb," said Supercat. "I'm not sleeping, anyway. I'm wondering what that funny noise is."

James could see that Supercat's ears were swivelling again.

"What funny noise?"

Supercat sat up.

"Can't you hear it? It sounds like

a herd of hippopotami snorting, wheezing, whistling and grunting. Do you think the palace has a Hippo Room?"

James shrugged. "Maybe. There are rooms for just about everything else. Where's the noise coming from?"

Supercat pointed to the West Tower, which overlooked the rose garden.

"Up there, top floor," he said. "My super-feline hearing is never wrong."

James didn't want to doubt Supercat, but something bothered him.

"If it's hippos, how could they

139

climb the spiral staircase? Wouldn't

they get stuck?"

Supercat thought about it for a

second.

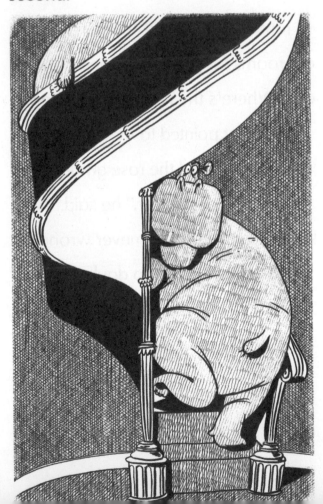

"In which case, they need rescuing!" he cried, leaping off the bed.

He ran out into the hall, then skidded to a halt and cupped his ear with his paw.

"What is it?" said James.

"It's... *snoring*!" said Supercat. "It sounded like hippopotami when we were in the Queen's bedroom, but from here I can tell it's the sound of many people sleeping, one of whom is snoring in an American accent."

"It must be the US President," said

141

James. "Well done, Supercat! Let's hurry to the tower. The hospital wing must be there."

Supercat and James ran up the stairs to the tower, passing a huge cannon on the way. It almost stopped Supercat in his tracks, but there was no time to lose. James tugged at his tail and they hurried to the top. By the time they got there, even James's normal human ears could hear the sound of snoring, loud and clear.

"I'm surprised no one's guarding the

door," he whispered as he peered through the tiny window of the hospital wing.

Supercat reached up to prod the entry buzzer.

"We can't just march in," said James. "The Count's men could be anywhere."

"Can you see the Queen?" asked Supercat.

"No," said James. "All the beds are behind curtains. There are lots of doctors, but they're not doing much. They're just lounging around drinking coffee."

Supercat pressed his nose to the glass and scanned them with his super-feline vision.

"They're not doctors, James. Look at their shoes. They have numbers on."

They were Calculators! Supercat and James ducked down.

"Why are they pretending to be doctors?" said Supercat.

"Think about it," said James. "If the patients wake up and find the hospital full of Calculators, they'll panic, won't they? They're world leaders – they

144

won't just lie back and let themselves
be imprisoned. They'll summon the
army to overthrow their captors."

There was a trolley near the door.
On the top shelf there were medical
instruments and a pile of doctor's

145

gowns. James put one on and slung a stethoscope round his neck.

"If I'm disguised as a doctor, I can mingle among the Calculators," he said, tying on a surgical mask. "They'll never know it's me."

"Is there one in my size?" said Supercat. There wasn't.

"Hide under that blanket on the bottom shelf of the trolley," said James. "I'll push you round the ward in secret. You can be my eyes and ears."

Supercat climbed on. James covered his tail and pressed the entry buzzer.

"Right, we're going in."

One of the 'doctors' looked up from the paper he was reading and, mistaking James for a Crew member, he pressed the button under the reception desk, let him in and went back to reading the sports page.

James pushed the trolley from cubicle to cubicle, peeking behind the curtains. The Duke and the princes were still snoring their heads off, and the princess had fallen asleep in her party frock. James hurried to the next bed and pulled back the curtain.

"Oh... Hellay!" said a posh voice.

"Your Majesty!" exclaimed James.

"Thank goodness you're awake."

The Queen rubbed her eyes.

"Where *is* one?" she said. "Why am
I wearing my ermine robe in bed?"

"You're in hospital, Your Highness," said James, lowering his voice. "I'm afraid there was an incident at your birthday feast."

The Queen blushed.

"An incident?" she said. "Did I fall off the table doing the cancan again?"

"It was no accident, ma'am," said James.

He sat on her bed and explained about the cake and the Count's plot to take over the world.

"I thought the icing tasted a bit orf," she said, straightening her tiara. "And you say Backwards is behind it? Last time, he tried to steal my crown jewels. Five, four, three, two, one has had quite enough of that nasty little man. I'm calling the army to get rid of him."

She reached for her handbag and

took out a mobile phone.

"Bother, it's gorn flat," she said. "Doctor, could you lend me yours?"

"My parents won't let me have a mobile until I'm eleven," said James.

The Queen put on her glasses and squinted at him.

"How old are you now?"

"Ten," said James. "It's my birthday today."

The Queen shook his hand.

"Same as mine! Many happy returns... I say, you're frightfully young for a doctor."

"I'm not a doctor," said James.
"I'm James Jones. Supercat and I have
come to rescue you."

Supercat threw back the blanket,
jumped off the trolley and bowed
before the Queen.

"Never fear, Supercat is here!"

"Is he?" said the Queen.

Supercat gave her a salute.

"Yes! Forget
the army, Your
Majesty. There's
nothing I can't
handle."

"Splendid!" said the Queen. "We need a plan. Could you possibly run along and wake the Prime Minister? Tell him Queenie said we need his help to get this country under control instantly. I am not having Backwards ruling Britannia! He'll make a pig's ear of it."

"Of course, right away," said James, slipping through the curtain.

Supercat was just about to follow, when the Queen grabbed his paw. "Ahem, before you go, would you mind awfully passing me that bedpan, Supercat? One is bursting for a royal wee."

Supercat did as he was told, then walked out to meet James, pulling a face.

"Well, you did say you could handle anything!" said James.

Chapter Seven

THUMP, WALLOP, BLINK!

"James set off to visit the other patients, steering the trolley ahead of him with Supercat safely hidden on the bottom shelf under the blanket. The Prime Minister was first on the list but while he was looking for him, James was stopped by one of the

Count's guards.

"Afternoon, comrade," said the Calculator. "Have you seen Backwards by any chance?"

Rather than blow his disguise by sounding like a child, James lowered his voice to what he hoped was a manly grunt and put on a cockney accent.

"Yeah, mate. I've seen him. He was sittin' on the throne trying on crowns."

He seemed to have got away with it – the Calculator became quite chatty.

"King for a day?" he scoffed. "Backwards couldn't rule a line, let alone a country."

"Too right, pal," said James, confident that his fake accent had fooled the Calculator. "I've got better things to do on my birthday than stand here watching posh sorts dribbling into their pillows."

The Calculator clapped him on the back.

"Many happy returns!" he said, "How old?"

"Ten," said James, instantly realising his mistake. His heart began to pound but to his relief, the Calculator thought it was a joke and chuckled.

"Well, you don't look it!" he said.

James laughed along with him, did a three-point turn with his trolley and quickly ducked behind the nearest curtain, only to find a large gentleman sitting up in bed, dressed in the national costume of Tonga.

"Good afternoon," said James. "I have come to rescue you."

He tried to explain the situation, but the King of Tonga just stared at him blankly.

"*Ikai mahino!*" he said.

"Sorry, I don't speak Tongan," said James. "But I know a cat who might."

Supercat could speak French, German, Spanish, Italian and Tiger. With any luck, he might know Tongan and be able to translate. James whipped off the blanket.

"*Ko hoku hingoa ko* Supercat!" said Supercat, shaking the king warmly by the hand. "*Oku ou lea faka-Tonga si is' ipe!*"

The king looked relieved and patted him on the head.

"What did you say to him?" asked James.

"I told him my name and mentioned that I could speak a little Tongan," said Supercat smugly. James was impressed.

"Amazing. Could you tell him what's happened please?"

Supercat nodded.

"*Si!*"

"And can you also tell him that I've got a plan to get everyone out of here?"

"*Non.*"

"Why not?" said James.

"Because I don't know what the plan is," said Supercat. "You haven't told me yet."

James apologised. "I only just came up with it. I think you'll like it," he said.

Supercat's eyes lit up.

"Does it involve pilchards?"

"Pillows," said James. "When all the guests are in on the plan, I'll set off the fire alarm to distract the Calculators. That's the cue for everyone to spring out of bed and fight them off with their pillows – with your help, of course."

Supercat grabbed a spare pillow in readiness.

"You're a genius, James Jones," he said. "Fur and feathers will fly! I will fight them off and tie them up with bandages."

"Good," said James. "You tell the King of Tonga and I'll tell all the others. Then Her Majesty can deal with the Count."

When James explained the plan to

the Prime Minister and the man from the Ministry of Defence, who were conveniently sleeping top to tail in the same bed, they were delighted.

CLAP CLAP

"We haven't had a good pillow fight since we shared a dorm at Eton, have we, sir?" said the man from the Ministry.

"What larks!" said the Prime Minister. "I can't wait to give Backwards a biffing!"

James dashed off to bring the US President up to speed, but when he told him about the pillow fight, his mind seemed elsewhere.

"Dang!" he sighed.

"Are you worried my plan won't work?" said James. "Only there are more of us than there are of them and they're very good pillows."

"Heck no," said the President. "It's not that. I've left my darn party bag in the Banqueting Hall. It had my favourite candy in too. I bet Backwards has eaten it."

"I doubt it," said James, picturing the Count swaddled in bunting. "He's a bit tied up at the moment. But when we go and arrest him we can get your party bag too."

James dodged in and out of the curtains telling the other royals to prepare for battle.

Then it was only the Queen left, and when he told her the plan, she was keener than anybody.

"Spiffing!" she snorted. "It will be even more fun than the time one put a drawing pin on the Pope's chair."

When everyone was ready, James tiptoed over to the fire alarm and smashed the glass with his fist.

BRRRRRRRRRRRRRRRRRRRing!

"Fire!" shouted James. "Fire!"

The Calculators looked round in panic and headed for the exit, only to be met by a mob of angry royals, led by Supercat, running towards them with pillows.

"Tiger Power, rargh, rargh rargh!

Take *that!*" yelled Supercat.

BIFF! THWACK! POUF!

Now the President and the Prime Minister were attacking the Calculators from behind.

PHLUMP! WALLOP! BINK!

"You're a disgrace to the National Health Service!" shouted the Prime Minister as his pillow exploded over a bogus doctor in a cloud of goose down.

"Good shot, sir!" yelled the man from the Ministry. "Right on the bonce!"

The Queen seemed to be
enjoying the battle enormously. She
had already defeated six Calculators
and although she was older than
James's grandma, she was going for
her seventh.

Ten minutes later, it was all over.
Her Majesty swung her pillow at the

last man standing, knocked him
down and sat on him while Supercat
span round him with bandages, like
a spider wrapping up an enormous
fly. By now, all the Calculators were
wriggling helplessly on the floor. James
dusted himself down, cleared the
feathers from his throat and gave a

triumphant whoop.

"Woo hoo! Well done, everybody! You can all go home now."

"Hurrah!" said the Queen. "Thank you all for coming – especially

those who flew over in their private jets from... I say! Where is the US President?"

He was nowhere to be seen.

"Hmm, he may have gone to get

his party bag, Your Majesty," said James.

As well as his favourite candy, the President had specifically mentioned a miniature set of furry dice that he wanted to hang in his plane for the ride home from the palace.

"Oh, the party bags!" said the Queen. "One almost forgot..."

"Let's get them now, and bag Count Backwards at the same time."

"That's twice we've beaten Count Backwards, James!" said Supercat

proudly as they followed the Queen
out of the hospital wing and down
the spiral staircase to the Banqueting
Hall. They had just run past the huge
cannon when suddenly something
caught James's eye through a
window.

"Oh no, you may have spoken
too soon," he frowned. "Look...
Backwards!"

Supercat looked behind him.

"I can't see anything," he said.

"No, look through there!" said
James, pointing outside.

"It's Count Backwards, he's kidnapping the US President!"

The Queen polished her glasses and peered out.

"That's very naughty!" she scolded, rapping on the window to try and get the Count's attention. "Stop it this instant, you beastly little man!"

Supercat watched in horror as Mr Plus and Mr Minus bundled the struggling President into his own jet.

"How did they escape?" said Supercat, thrashing his tail.

"More importantly, how are we
going to stop them?" said James.

"Even at super-speed, you can't outrun the jet from here. By the time you get to the ground floor, Count Backwards will have taken off."

"Can't you fly, Supercat?" asked the Queen.

James was about to say no on his behalf, when Supercat had a brainwave.

"Yes, Your Majesty," he said. "Like a cannonball..."

And before James could stop him, Supercat ran back up the stairs to the armoury...

Chapter Eight
CALL ME SIR

James ran after Supercat, closely followed by the Queen, who had kicked off her party shoes so she could keep up.

"What did Supercat mean when he said he could fly like a cannonball?" she asked.

But when they got to the armoury, James didn't have to explain. Supercat had climbed into the cannon. James could see his whiskers poking out of the barrel.

"Are you mad?" said James.

"I'm furious!" said Supercat. "I am not letting Count Backwards get away. Open the window, light the fuse and fire me into the President's jet."

The aeroplane was already cruising along the grass outside the palace, preparing for take-off.

"It's too dangerous," said James.

"I can't let you do it."

Supercat twiddled his thumbs
impatiently.

"It's nice that you care, but a cat's
gotta do what a cat's gotta do."

Which was worse, thought James. *World Domination by Backwards or losing the best pet in the world?* It was a no-brainer.

"I haven't got any matches," he said stubbornly.

The Queen fiddled about in her handbag.

"I have, I used them to light my birthday cake. There aren't many left – one had a frightful lot of candles – but there are two."

She handed James the matchbox. He handed them back.

"Sorry," he said. "I'm not allowed to play with matches."

"I am!" said Her Majesty cheerily. "I can do what I like, I'm Queen."

The jet was roaring along the grass now, its nose beginning to lift.

"You won't be for much longer, if Backwards gets his way!" said Supercat. "Fire me out of this cannon now if you want me to save your country."

"Don't do it. Please," said James.

"Don't be a wuss," said the Queen, opening the window and striking the first match. To James's relief, a gust of wind puffed it out.

Then he realised – maybe he *was* being a wuss. This wasn't just any old pet puss – this was Supercat!

"One sec…" he said, running over to the collection of ancient armour arranged on the wall. He grabbed a tiny helmet that must have belonged to a baby knight and slipped it over Supercat's head.

"Health and safety," said James. "Good luck!"

The Queen turned away from the

draught, struck the last match and lit the fuse. As it fizzed and sparked, James pointed the cannon up at the jet, which had taken off and was climbing up into the clouds.

"God save the Queen!" said Supercat.

BOOOOOOOM!

James watched as his furry sidekick
shot out of the cannon, soared
through the sky and smashed through
the jet window into the cockpit,
helmet first.

"Bravo!" said the Queen. "Supercat should be very proud of that manoeuvre."

"I'm not sure that he will," said James, pulling something out of the smoking cannon. "He's left his pants behind."

James would have loved to see Count Backwards' face when Supercat blasted through the clouds into his cabin. He'd run out into the palace grounds with the Queen to get a better view, and although they could see the plane, it was too high to see what was going on inside. It seemed to be going up and down rather a lot, and rocking about, as if a struggle was taking place.

"I do hope Supercat will be tickety-boo," said the Queen. "One isn't a fan of cats normally, but one has to admire him – so brave! I've grown very fond of him."

"Me too," said James, wishing he was by Supercat's side.

Suddenly, there was a loud *pop* and a *whoosh*. James watched in disbelief as Count Backwards shot out through the roof of the jet. He fell through the sky, flapping his arms like a startled vulture, then disappeared from view.

"Good grief!" exclaimed the Prime Minister. "Supercat must have pressed the ejector button."

"Yes!" cried James, punching the air. "Well done, Supercat!"

The plane did a victory roll in the air and then landed safely.

"Good cat!" said the man from the Ministry of Defence. "He deserves a medal."

"One shall see to it instantly," said

the Queen as Supercat helped the President out of the jet.

James ran over to congratulate him.

"You were brilliant," he said.

Supercat took off his helmet and was about to agree when he looked down and realised that something was missing.

"I was— oh, *pants!*" he blushed.

"One doesn't care if you're wearing pants or not, Supercat," said the Queen as he knelt before her throne. "It's what's underneath that counts. You have saved this country and the world from an evil villain, for which one is truly grateful."

She stood up and touched him lightly on his shoulder with a ceremonial sword.

"For showing great daring and courage, I knight you Sir Supercat. Arise!"

There was a thunderous round of applause from all the party guests as Sir Supercat stood up. James was clapping so loudly, he didn't hear the Queen call out his own name.

"James Jones... Master James Jones?"

The King of Tonga gave him a nudge.

"Yes, Your Majesty?"

"Step forward, please."

James went and stood next to Supercat. He was so excited, he was

shaking. The Queen was holding a
gold medal.

"My loyal subjects," she said,
"behind every great cat, there is a
great boy and as you have seen by
his actions today, James is one of
the finest."

She walked forward.

"James Jones, it gives me great
pleasure to award you the Queen's
Gold Medal for your part in bringing
down Count Backwards. You may not
have flown the plane, but you are the
driving force behind Team Supercat

and for that, we take our hats orf
to you!"

The guests threw their party
crowns in the air as she pinned the
medal to his chest.

"Thank you!" said James proudly.
The Queen held up her finger.

"One more thing before you go..." she said, reaching into her robe pocket for something. It was a light-up birthday badge. She pinned it next to his medal.

"Happy Birthday, James. You must come to my party next year with Sir Supercat. Look out for your invitations in the post."

As the guests sang 'Happy Birthday', James's heart swelled with pride. But nothing made him prouder than when Supercat whispered three little words to him:

"Well done, us!"

James would have loved to stay
longer and show off his gold medal
a bit more. After all, he wouldn't be
able to wear it at home. He wasn't

meant to have been at the palace. He was meant to have been at the zoo, with the zookeeper. James looked at his watch. It was 5.30.

"Oh no!" he gasped. "I promised to meet my family by the zoo gift shop at six. We're going to be really late."

Happily, the US President was so grateful for being rescued that he made them an offer they couldn't refuse – a lift back to the zoo in his private jet.

They landed in Regent's Park with five minutes to spare. James took

off his gold medal and gave it to
Supercat.

"Look after it for me," he said. "See
you at the station. Safe journey."

Supercat gave what was left of his
cloak an extra-dramatic swish.

"May I remind you that I'm *Sir*
Supercat now!"

James straightened his mask for
him.

"Like I could forget the best
birthday ever!" he said. "That's the
last party Count Backwards will
poop on."

They slapped their palms together in triumph.

"High five, four, three, two, one!" said Supercat.

EPILOGUE

As James ran to meet his parents, preparing all the lies he was going to have to tell about the wonderful day he'd had at the zoo, somewhere in the grounds of Buckingham Palace, a twisted, tattooed figure dangled from a treetop by his parachute, cursing the crows and a certain tubby tabby.

"If I ever get down alive, I will find you, Supercat!" he screeched. "And when I do, I will make you call me 'Sir.'

HAVE YOU READ:

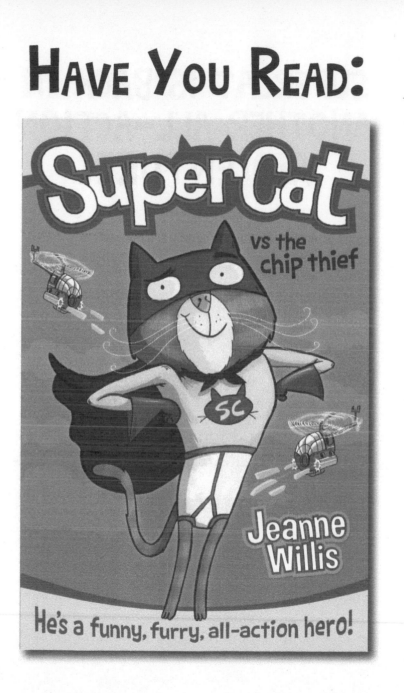

SUPERCAT IS BACK IN ANOTHER ALL-ACTION ADVENTURE!

Tiger was an ordinary pet, until the day he licked a toxic sock and was transformed into… **SUPERCAT!**

All the grown-ups are missing and Supercat and James suspect the evil Count Backwards is behind it. Can they sneak on board his submarine and save the day or will they end up as fish food?

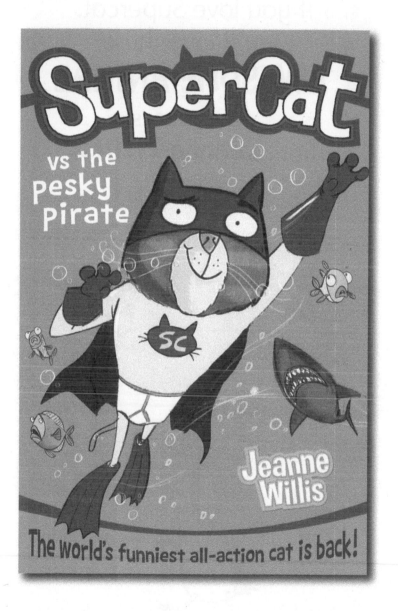

If you love Supercat,
you'll love these
AWESOME ANIMAL
adventures
from **Jeanne Willis:**